Trellis Publishing, Inc.

P.O. Box 16141
Duluth, MN 55816
1-800-513-0115

Honk: The Moose

Story by Phil Stong, Pictures by Kurt Wiese
Biwabik Special Edition

Publisher's Cataloging-in-Publication
(Provided by Quality Books, Inc.)

Stong, Phil, 1899-1957.
    Honk the moose / by Phil Stong ; illustrated by Kurt
Wiese — Biwabik special ed.
    p. cm.
    SUMMARY: Two young boys discover a moose wandering around their town and name him "Honk" for the sound he continually makes. Based on a true story.
    Audience: Ages 8-12
    LCCN 2001-087156
    ISBN 1-930650-36-1

    1. Moose–Juvenile fiction. 2. Minnesota–Juvenile fiction. [1. Moose–Fiction. 2. Minnesota–Fiction.] I. Wiese, Kurt, 1887- II. Title.
PZ7.S883Ho 2001   [Fic]
                    QBI01-700239

Printed in the United States of America
First printing: April, 2001
10 9 8 7 6 5 4 3 2

HONK: THE MOOSE

HONK: THE MOOSE

Story By

PHIL STONG

Pictures By

KURT WIESE

Introduction

Honk: The Moose is a wonderful children's book based on a true story about two boys who discover a moose in their community. The actual setting of the story is Biwabik, Minnesota. While working as a teacher and coach in Biwabik from 1919-1920, author Phil Stong learned the story of Honk from those who later became characters in the book. Eugenia and Louis Pagnucco, Ivar Riise, Waino Karkinen, and others mentioned in the book were actual residents who still have family members living in Biwabik. In fact, Archie Milner, the grocer Honk visited, was my great uncle.

This beloved story was once used by one of Biwabik's dedicated schoolteachers, Lois Moeller, as a regular part of her curriculum. As a result, it became part of the City's heritage. For generations the story of Honk has been passed on in the oral tradition. We are excited to have *Honk: The Moose* available in print, once again, to share with our families, friends and visitors.

We open our hearts as we welcome you to come to Biwabik, a now beautifully renovated Alpine golf and ski village, where you can take a moment to visit our life-size statue of Honk standing in the park where he once followed Ivar and Waino.

I dedicate this edition to the past and present citizens of Biwabik, who have kept the legend alive, and to my wife, Kathy, for understanding my dreams and supporting me in reprinting *Honk: The Moose*.

Steve Bradach, Mayor of Biwabik
Home of *Honk: The Moose*

CONTENTS

Chapter I

HUNTER

WAINO and Ivar had been hunting all day but they had not found any deer—not even a bear. Ivar was pretty certain that he had shot a rabbit with his thousand-shooting air gun but the rabbit was pretty sure he hadn't. They slid down the rolling hills above Birora, Minnesota, on their hickory skis and started the slow tramp, on foot, up the brick streets.

All the hills of the Iron Range are made of red or purple iron ore and covered thickly with evergreens—fir, spruce, cedar. The roads are red with iron ore in the summer and green with trees; in the long winter of that northern country they are white and green.

Ivar's hair was so light that it was almost white. He had smiled so much in the ten years of his life that two small smile wrinkles had set up business at the corners of his eyes to make it easier for him. Waino had dark, stubbly hair and his head was almost as round as a basketball. Whatever Ivar thought suited Waino.

"If we had shot a deer," Ivar said, "I guess he would have been pretty hard to get home."

Waino nodded. "Couldn't have done it. Anyway, deers are pretty nice—they don't hurt anybody."

[7]

They had put their skis over their shoulders and the ice that had
formed on Waino's ski, where the snow had piled up under his toe, fell off
at this time—into the collar of his mackinaw jacket.

"Here, you," he told the ski. "That'll be enough of that."

"Well, g'bye, Ivar—I might as well turn in here."

"Oh come on down to the stable. We'll oil the skis and sit in the hay."

Ivar's father kept the livery stable in Birora. He boarded the horses and the donkeys from the iron mines and the horses from the lumber camps. He was a doctor, too, and took care of them when they were sick.

Waino thought it over. "All right. We'll plan where we're going to hunt tomorrow." He pinged the air rifle at a fence and hit part of it. "Wish that had been a good old moose," he said.

He didn't mean it. A moose is considerably bigger than a very big horse and its antlers are about the size of the kitchen stove. While an air gun is a very dangerous weapon and will make almost anyone jump and yell, it would not make a moose jump and yell. The moose might notice that it had been shot or it might not. If it did notice, the two boys would have had to climb a tree, or two trees, as soon as possible.

"We could have put his horns over the fireplace," Ivar said.

They were getting rather cold. Their fathers and mothers had come to America and to the Iron Range from Finland, which is a good deal closer to the North Pole than to Minnesota; but even here the thermometer was thirty degrees below zero and the cold wind blew up over the Missabe Hills from Lake Superior.

[11]

It was good to get into the warm stable and up close to the hot stove in the office.

"Papa must have had to drive somewhere," Ivar said, opening his jacket to the warmth of the stove. He got a rag and a can of harness oil and the two boys began to rub down their skis to keep the wood from warping or wearing.

"I still wish," Waino said dreamily, "that that had been a good old moose I shot."

Ivar dropped his skis and seized the air gun. "If that had been a moose," he said, "this is what I'd have done to him." He fired three shots, as fast as he could pull the lever, out the door of the office and down the dark corridor between the stalls where the horses were feeding.

There was a very sad sound at once. It went "Haawwnnk—hawnk—hawnk—haawwnnkk!"

The two boys dropped the air gun, oil, skis, rags—everything. "Golly gee! What do you think that is, Ivar?"

Ivar had jumped straight up in the air, but not as high as nine feet. He was brave again now—he was fairly sure he was. "It—it sounded—it sounded like an automobile."

"Automobiles don't care if you shoot them," Waino suggested.

"Might have hit the honker."

"It honked a long time."

"Yeah." Ivar admitted that it was not an automobile. He braced his shoulders back. He was a Suomi—*Swho-me*—which is what brave Finlanders call themselves. He remembered Vainamoinen, the Finnish hero, just as good as Hiawatha and Columbus and Daniel Boone. "I'll find out what it is."

He went bravely to the light switch that lit up the long aisles of the barn.

"Maybe it was a moose," Waino said softly. He came over and looked across Ivar's shoulder.

Ivar pressed the switch.

[13]

It *was* a moose.

Chapter II

HONK

IT was a sad moose. It was, very likely, the saddest moose there had ever been.

That was the coldest winter Minnesota had had in a great many years. The grass, the moss that a moose eats, were under seven feet of snow and over the snow there was a thick coat of sleet and ice. Deer nibbled tree branches for food. The moose was sad because he was very hungry.

He had looked everywhere for a breakfast that was three days late. At last, when he had just about decided that there *weren't* any more breakfasts, he had come to an odd place in the woods—which was Birora, though he didn't know it—and fortunately had come into town on the livery stable side. His trained nose had told him that here were all the breakfasts, lunches and dinners that he had missed for the past month. So, it *was* a moose.

Ivar shut the door of the office quickly. "Nothing," he said. "Just a moose." He thoughtfully slipped the bolt on the door.

Waino's eyes grew round and his knees shook a little. "Oh," he said faintly, "Just a moose?"

They stood there for a while, thinking about a good many things. "I suppose I'd better go out and shoot him—after while," Ivar said.

Waino caught his arm, although he did not need to because Ivar had not started for the door. In fact, he had kept as far away from it as possible. "That moose isn't hurting us. He isn't even making any noise. Besides, I think I've got to go home—Mama probably wants me to do something."

"Oh," said Ivar, brightly, "that's fine then. You can shoot him as you go by. I better stay here in case the telephone rings."

"I guess I can stay a little while," Waino said.

They sat for a long time and said nothing, but Ivar was thinking all the time. The more he thought, the more he began to get mad, and then he began to get madder and madder. When a Finn gets mad he doesn't do a halfway job. First he gets madder than a Chinaman; then he works up through the Italians and the French and on to the English and the Germans

and *then* to the Irish—and when he is madder than a mad Norwegian he knows that he is a real Suomi.

"That moose hasn't any business in my Papa's livery stable," Ivar said firmly. "I'm going out and teach him a lesson." This was a very bad thing for him to say. "Teaching people a lesson" usually means that you teach them what a bad temper you have. Ivar had some right to be angry now—he was cheerful and quiet most of the time—but he was being locked up in his own father's office by a moose. That would upset anyone.

"Maybe—there might be some other meeses," Waino objected dimly, as Ivar started to open the door.

"I'll teach them all a lesson," Ivar told him, and marched out. Of course, Waino had to go with him.

Ivar marched steadily down the long, dim-lit corridor. He knew that it was very likely that if he ever quit marching he would turn around and run as fast as he could, so he kept bravely putting one foot in front of the other—Tramp, Tramp, Tramp—past the stalls where the horses were munching uneasily. It seemed to the horses that there was some very queer sort of horse in the place.

It didn't make Ivar feel any better to hear Waino's feet going Sloosh, Sloosh, Sloosh on tiptoe instead of Tramp, Tramp, Tramp.

And there was the moose, lots bigger than the biggest cow there ever was, with his great spreading antlers, something like the branches on a flat cactus, except that each branch was about the size of a scoop-shovel.

The moose glanced up at them and then went on filling himself as full as he could of Ivar's father's expensive hay.

"You get out of here," Ivar scolded. "You haven't got any business eating our hay. Get out! Right away!"

[19]

The moose paid no attention whatever. He was still very sad but not as sad as he had been.

"I told you to get out," Ivar said and he went and poked the moose in the ribs.

The moose turned his head slowly. "Hawwn-n-k-k," he said, but the boys did not hear the end of this plainly because they were locked up in the office again. They waited there for a moment, listening.

"I guess I showed that moose a few things," Ivar said bravely and then he jumped clear out of his chair. Something was rattling the door—the doorknob turned!

Chapter III

WHAT DO YOU DO WITH A MOOSE?

WAINO was in the corner between Papa's desk and the wall. Ivar knew, really, that the air gun wouldn't kill a moose. He picked up a pitchfork and went bravely to the door.

The doorknob twisted again. "You get away from there," Ivar shouted. "Go on back in the woods where you belong."

There was a pause. "What's the matter in there? Why's the door locked?"

"Papa!" Ivar said, and threw back the bolt.

Ivar's father was not fat but he was about as big as two men. His face was all pink and white and his eyes were as good-humored as Ivar's. He smiled at the two boys, now.

"What's the matter?" he asked again. "You look like you yust seen a ghost." Because he had spoken only Finnish and Swedish as a boy, it was still hard for him to say "J." He said "Y" instead. Ivar, who was an American boy, said "J" but he never noticed that his father said "Y." He had always heard him speak that way.

"A moose," Ivar said.

"A moose," Waino added.

"What!" Then Ivar's father laughed and the floor shook a little. "You yust seen a moose, what? Well, he wouldn't chase you here."

"Out in the stable," Ivar told him.

Ivar's father laughed a good deal and everything shook. "A moose in the stable. I think you've got a bat in the belfry, Ivar. I guess a horse got loose. You go up and see if your mother has any errands—I'll take care of the moose."

"It's a moose, Papa—honestly!"

"You should see things straight, Ivar," his father said. "A Suomi should see things straight. It is a horse, and because you were afraid you say it is a moose. Come on, we'll see this moose, now. A Suomi should not be afraid, either—"

He opened the door and stepped out into the aisle. "We will see."

An instant afterward he scooped the two boys up in his strong hands and almost threw them back into the office. He followed them and locked the door. "It's a moose," he said.

[22]

Ivar's father thought for a moment and then the same stubborn bravery that had made Ivar go out against the moose made his father rise and go to the door. "You lock the door after me and stay here. We'll see about this. If I call, you go out the window and run for the policeman."

He opened the door and went out, but Ivar disobeyed. He was not going to let his father talk to a moose unless he was there to help. He walked out quietly behind his father, so, of course, Waino went too.

The moose had eaten so much hay that he was growing sleepy. He still nibbled at the hay, which he could just reach as it hung over from the loft, but he didn't want it very much. Only, since the hay was there, he might as well eat it while he had the chance.

"Wonderful!" said Ivar's father. "How could anything eat so much? You please shoo now," he added to the moose.

[24]

Honk rolled one eye toward him and went on eating. This made Ivar's father angry. "Hay costs twenty dollars a ton. You have already eaten a ton. How do you pay?" In fact, the moose had stuffed himself with hay, after the long, hungry days in the woods, until he looked like a balloon that had been blown up only at the front end. The other end was still skinny.

"It's honestly—"

"Yes, I know," Ivar's father interrupted him. "It's a moose. How he got here, I don't know."

"The winter is bad—maybe he was cold."

Ivar's father smiled at Waino, at the same time keeping an eye on the moose. "Not cold—mooses don't care if it is cold. But I guess he was hungry. He must have come here in the afternoon when nobody was looking."

"What are you going to do with him, Mr. Ketonen?" Waino asked

[25]

eagerly. For a young boy he always showed a very practical mind.

"What am I going to do with him?" Ivar's father said, a little bit crossly. "What does one do with a moose? I am going to do what one always does with mooses."

"What's that?" Ivar asked curiously.

"I am going to shoo him out of my barn. What will the horses think?"

"What *will* they, Papa?"

"They will think I don't keep a good livery stable. Mooses!"

At this moment Honk's legs collapsed. He felt very good, but tired. He rolled one eye at the people and then he sank on his side and rolled himself once or twice. After that, with a contented sigh, he went to sleep.

This made Ivar's father angry again. "You get out of here. You can't sleep here." He prodded the moose in the side. Honk did not even open his eyes.

Ivar began to feel a little sorry for the moose. He could see how sleepy the animal was and he thought of mornings when he had had to get up to go to school in spite of the fact that he was having a splendid time sleeping.

"I wish I was mean enough to stick him with a pitchfork," Ivar's father said unhappily. "Listen, you!" he said fiercely to the moose. "If you don't go away I'll get the policeman; and do you know what he'll do to you? He'll shoot you."

The moose did not open his eyes even then. He said "HAAAWNK" very softly and sleepily.

"All right," said Mr. Ketonen firmly. "Ivar, you go for the policeman."

"Aw, Papa—!"

"Aw, Mr. Ketonen—!" said Waino.

[27]

"Can I run a livery barn with a moose in it? He'll eat me out of house and home. He'll get in the way. Besides, mooses are dangerous."

"That one isn't, Papa. Look at him."

"How do we know what he'll be like when he wakes up? You go get the policeman, Ivar."

"All right."

Ivar and Waino left the stable. Night had fallen—it was almost supper-time—and the bright corner lights of the little mining town twinkled and glittered on the snowy streets. They found Mr. Ryan, the policeman, in the mayor's office, over the fire station. His belt with its two enormous revol-

vers was hung from a nail on the wall. He was reading the evening paper.

He merely glanced over the edge of the paper at Ivar and Waino.

"Well," he said severely, " I knew when I saw you start out with that gun you'd get into trouble. What've you done? Killed a moose hunting out of season—or maybe several mooses?"

The boys knew that this was a joke, but they were too breathless to laugh.

"Papa wants you to come put a moose out of his livery stable."

Mr. Ryan liked to joke. He stared at them for a moment and then he frowned.

"Playing jokes on an officer of the law, uh? I'll just take you back to the jail and let you pick your rooms right now. And remember," he said slowly, "what we have here for supper is bread and water—and that's what we have for breakfast and for dinner."

"No, Mr. Ryan, please, it isn't a joke. Papa wants you to come put a moose out his livery stable."

"No, Mr. Ryan, please, it isn't a joke—" Waino said.

Mr. Ryan grinned and reached for his belt. For a minute he'd thought the boys were trying to make him believe a real moose was in the stable and then he remembered that "moose" was Minnesota slang for a big man.

It was pretty late for tramps up on the Iron Range and, anyway, Ivar Ketonen (young Ivar was named for his father) was about as big a "moose" himself as anyone would want to see. He wasn't the kind that would ask for help or need it, usually.

At the same time, if Ketonen needed help he might need it pretty badly. Mr. Ryan started at a swift walk that made the boys trot. Mr. Ryan

[30]

was a small Irishman but he was very strong and braver than he was strong.

"What's this moose doing?" he asked Ivar.

"He's asleep, Mr. Ryan."

Mr. Ryan laughed. "We'll give him a better place to sleep up here in the jail. Did he make any trouble?"

"No, he just ate a lot of—"

[32]

"Oh, broke into the house, uh? Well, that's bad." Mr. Ryan grew serious. "He oughtn't to have done that. We'd have fed him and let him go tomorrow. Now, I guess, we'll have to keep him. That's bad—breaking into places."

"Yes, sir," Ivar said anxiously.

"He steal anything?"

[33]

"No, sir. Just a lot of—"

"Nothing but food, poor fellow. Well, we'll see what we can do for him. He must have been mighty hungry. Didn't know enough to come around to me. I'd have fed him and given him a bed. He might be all right after all." Mr. Ryan hated to arrest people—he hated to see them get into trouble. But he wasn't afraid to arrest *anybody* if he thought he deserved to be in trouble.

Waino said timidly, "He's a kind of a sad moose, Mr. Ryan."

Mr. Ryan sighed. "Poor fellow. Hungry and just saw a door open, I suppose. It's been a hard winter. We'll see what we can do."

They had come to the door of the livery stable. Mr. Ryan believed the boys when they said the "moose" was sad but he didn't know how much they knew about tramps. He hooked his thumb over the edge of his belt close to one of the revolvers and opened the door quickly.

"Ivar?" Mr. Ryan called to Ivar's father.

"Frank?"

"Everything all right?"

"Everything is not all right. What are you going to do about this moose? What's he doing here?"

Mr. Ryan walked quickly and boldly down the aisle. The boys heard him gasp. "It's a moose!"

"I said it was a moose," Ivar told him. He added, rather anxiously, "What are you going to do with him, Mr. Ryan?"

Waino said, "What are you going to do with him, Mr. Ryan?"

Chapter IV

WHAT *CAN* YOU DO WITH A MOOSE?

 ONK was not sad now, but he still *seemed* sad because his face was naturally sad. He was stuffed as full as he could be and he was in a comfortable place to sleep. That is about all that mooses worry about. Honk had been cold and hungry for so many days that he was not caught up on his sleep. One night, too, there had been wolves that he had had to drive away. The snow had

been so deep and the crust on it so hard that he had hardly been able to get a good bite of grass for a month.

At last he had been so unhappy that he had forgotten the old Moose rule about keeping away from where People are. In fact, he had even forgotten about People. He had just walked ahead and ahead, hoping that there was still some grass somewhere—when he had seen flat trees—which was how he thought of boards—right together with a lot of grass among them. What People call a barn.

And he ate so much that he went to sleep. He knew he had gone to sleep because he had several dreams about People, but, young as he was—he had just reached his full growth—he knew they were just dreams and only honked at them once or twice.

Mr. Ryan prodded the moose with the toe of his shoe but Honk did not move. He was too sound asleep now even to honk.

"How'd he get in here?" Mr. Ryan looked at Ivar and Waino as if he thought that they might have brought him in.

[39]

"He was yust here," said Ivar's father. "Why did you let him in?"

"I don't go around looking for meese—mooses," Mr. Ryan answered. "I'm not supposed to look for them. I got plenty to do without looking for mooses."

Mr. Ketonen lifted his shoulders. "He is a hay-stealer. Are you a policeman or are you a policeman? Do you watch out for stealers?"

"I didn't know he was going to steal your hay, even if I'd seen him. I can't arrest everybody I see just because they *might* steal something. Can I?" he asked the boys.

"No, sir," they said, together.

Ivar's father and the policeman laughed, but Ivar's father looked at the moose and it was plain that he was worried. "Something must be done with him. Hay, it costs lots, and what will he do when he wakes up?"

Mr. Ryan scratched his head. "I guess the only thing to do is shoot him. I can't herd mooses." He took out one of his revolvers and looked at the cartridges. "I don't like to do it, though."

Ivar thought that this was a very bad idea, and so did Waino. "You can't shoot a poor moose when he's asleep. Anyway, see—he looks like he was about to cry."

"Yes, he looks like he was about to cry," Waino said.

"He does look kind of peaked," Mr. Ryan said, doubtfully. He put the revolver back and nudged the moose once or twice, thoughtfully. "Skinny as a rail. Poor old boy, he just saw a lot of hay and he didn't know it belonged to anybody—"

"He can have the hay," said Ivar's father, "but Yumping Yee—the horses won't like it! And what's going to happen when he wakes up?"

[41]

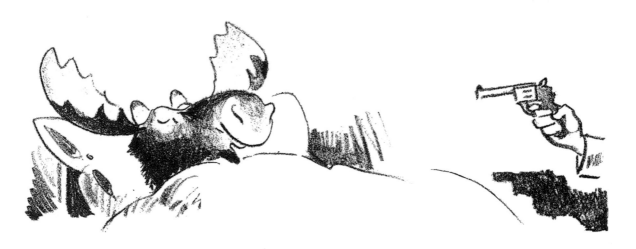

"It's not fair to shoot a moose when he's asleep," said Ivar again. He and Waino had begun to feel very sorry for Honk.

"That's right." Mr. Ryan hitched up his belt. "You see how he behaves when he wakes up, Ivar. If he acts mean, then maybe you could shoot him."

"If he acts mean," Mr. Ketonen said, "somebody should shoot me. I got twenty-two horses here, counting the mules. I don't want mooses running around my stable. And what about the hay?"

Mr. Ryan smiled but he did not let Mr. Ketonen see him. He knew that Ivar's father had a softer heart, almost, than anyone in Birora. That was why he had chosen to be a doctor for animals. "All right, Ivar—here's the revolver—you shoot him."

Ivar's father jumped quickly away from the revolver. "Me? I didn't say anything about shooting him. I asked you to come here please and take a moose out of my stable. Are you the police, here, or what are you?"

"I'm only the police for men. Meese—I mean mooses—there wasn't a single one of them voted for me or elected me marshal."

Ivar's father thought about this. "Ha—ha," he said, "this is my stable

[42]

—a *man* stable. If you can't take the moose away, then take the stable away from the moose."

"I tell you," said Ryan, "I guess we better call the mayor."

Chapter V

CITY COUNCIL

MR. NELS OLAVSSON, the Mayor of Birora, had been having a good supper. There was soup with all kinds of vegetables and lots of soup meat to eat with horse-radish; there was a whitefish from Lake Superior, and cream sauce; there were potatoes boiled with the jackets on and spinach with oil and vinegar dressing and some of his wife's canned tomatoes; and there would have been mince pie—but the telephone rang.

While he was gone Mama brought the hot mince pie to their three daughters—twelve, nine and five—and put a piece at Mr. Olavsson's place.

When he came back they all looked up together and they saw that he was putting on his mackinaw and his fur hat. The three little girls with their yellow hair quit eating pie and looked at their father, but it was Mama who asked, "What happened, Papa?"

[45]

"Nothing," he said, "but Mister Ryan has gone crazy and I must go down and see what I can do."

"*Mister Ryan?* Eat your pie, Papa. Mister Ryan wouldn't go crazy."

"He has gone crazy," Mayor Olavsson said firmly, pulling on his furry mittens. "He asked me to come down to Ivar Ketonen's because there was a moose in the stable."

"Can I come and see the moose?" Gunda asked. She was nine.

"I want to see the moose," said Christine, the youngest. "You never took me to see a moose, Papa."

"A moose in a livery stable!" said Olga, who was twelve. "There aren't any mooses in livery stables. They're in the woods. Can I come and see him too, Papa?"

"No—because the moose is in Mr. Ryan's head. It isn't a real moose. There wouldn't be a moose in a stable."

"Your pie is getting cold," Mama warned.

"I don't know when I'll be back," Mr. Olavsson said and hurried out.

Mrs. Olavsson put the pie back in the stove to keep warm. Mr. Olavsson walked down the street as fast as a fat man could. The snow puffed out like little fountains in front of his boots.

"Hello, Ivar," he called cautiously at the door of the livery stable.

"Hello, Nels." Then he heard Mr. Ryan call in the same tone of voice he always used, "Hello, Nels. Come on in."

The Mayor went in very slowly and he left the door off the latch so that he could get out again quickly. "Now, Frank," he said, "let's let the moose go and you come with me to the doctor—"

"Let the moose go!" Mr. Ryan said. "I'm not holding the moose. I wish he would go. I'd give anything if he'd go. You come let him go."

He was so mad that Mr. Olavsson was pretty sure he wasn't crazy. He went on down the aisle of the livery stable. "What's this moose you're talking about—did you say moose or mouse?"

"*Mouse,*" Mr. Ryan said grimly as the Mayor drew nearer.

Mr. Olavsson saw Honk. "My goodness! That's not a mouse—that's a *moose!*"

"Oh, you don't mean it!" Mr. Ryan said.

"But—what's he doing here?"

Mr. Ryan looked all over Honk. "Maybe he's learning to play the piano—or maybe he's knitting—or maybe he's reading a good book—but it looks to me like he was just sleeping."

[48]

Ivar felt that he had known this moose a long time now and he laughed. Waino laughed. The mayor frowned at them.

"I mean—how did he get here?"

Ivar's papa shook but he did not open his mouth to laugh. "I didn't have any moose so I had him sent by mail."

Mr. Olavsson did not even smile at this. "Just wandered in?"

"Yust wandered in," Ivar's father said.

"What are you going to do with him?"

Ivar's father shrugged his shoulders. "It's not *my* moose. This is the town moose. If it isn't, why is it in the town? If it is, why do you send it in to eat almost more than a ton of hay?"

[49]

Ivar and Waino were sitting on the moose and Mr. Ryan and Ivar's father were standing toward one end of him.

"He looks kind of skinny and he looks kind of like he doesn't feel good," Mr. Olavsson said. "Poor old Moose—it's been a hard winter."

"He was hungry," Ivar said.

"I can see," the Mayor said. "Why didn't you shoot him?"

"You can't shoot a moose when he's asleep," Mr. Ryan objected.

"No, don't shoot him," Ivar and Waino said together and they bounced up and down on the moose so much that it said "HAWWNK."

Mr. Ryan and Mr. Olavsson went into the office at once, but Ivar's father stayed and said: "Boys, your mothers might want you to run some errands. You better go on home while we figure this out."

"But they can't shoot poor old Honk," Ivar said, and though this was the moose's name, it was the first time anyone had mentioned it.

"No, they can't shoot poor old Honk," Waino said.

"We'll do what we think is best," Mr. Olavsson said crossly, from the office door.

"You aren't going to have him shot?" Mr. Ryan asked.

"No—we'll dispose of him."

When Ivar and Waino heard this they bounced up and down on Honk as hard as they could. They hoped he would wake up and go away before he was "disposed of" But Honk only said "H-H-H-AWWWWNNNK!" very slowly, without opening his eyes.

Ivar's father took a firm stand. "Me—I can't afford to feed a moose and I don't want him here. But I'd sooner see him here than disposed of. If this town won't take care of its mooses, I guess I'll have to."

[51]

Mr. Olavsson looked at Mr. Ryan, but anyone could see that Mr. Ryan was on Ivar Ketonen's side.

"I can't do this all by myself," the Mayor said. "I'll call the city council."

"You don't have to do that," Ivar's father said. "I shall at my own cost build a pen for him at once, until he tries to go away, and then I shall let him."

"No, Ivar," said the Mayor, unhappily, "you don't have to do that. I'll call the council and ask them what to do."

"One thing you will not do and that is to shoot that poor moose."

Five minutes later the same thing was happening in three different houses in Birora.

"Mr. Olavsson is clear crazy this time," said Mr. Lunn, snapping on his ear-muffs.

At the same time—"but think of it! The Mayor going out of his mind!"
Mr. Town Clerk Hulburd was saying to his family.

At the same time Mr. Councilman Hoaglund was shaking his head
sadly. "He shouldn't have worked so hard on the tax list. Think of it!
Mr. Olavsson kept saying and saying that there *was* a moose in the stable."

An hour later they were all sitting around a table in Ivar's father's office looking very puzzled.

"You can't shoot him—a sad moose like that," Mr. Olavsson was saying for the hundredth time.

"No—the poor fellow, he's starving!" Mr. Lunn said.

"You mean he *was* starving," Ivar's father corrected, thinking of his hay.

"I'll tell you," Mayor Olavsson said finally. "The town will pay for the hay and Frank can stay here tonight with his revolver. If the moose makes any fuss, then he must shoot him. But if he just goes away, everything will be all right."

They agreed on that. Sometime in the night Honk went quietly away.

Chapter VI

WINTER BOARDER

HE boys were still talking about the disaster when the mine whistle blew the next evening. A new boy, Jim Barry, whose father had just come to the Iron Range, had been skiing with them all afternoon down the sides of the waste dump —the long, narrow, sloping hill that is built up near a mine from the useless dirt dug out with the iron.

Jim Barry had been skiing only a small part of the time but he had been sliding all day—sometimes on his neck, sometimes on his chest, sometimes on his trousers but, since he had never been on skis before, only a small part of the time on his skis.

"I don't see how good old Honk could have gone off that way," Ivar said. "We always treated him right."

"Who named him Honk?" Jim Barry asked. He was feeling pretty good just then. He was beginning to get the feel of the skis and hadn't fallen down for fifty feet. But he turned his head to ask the question and when he took his next step he didn't know that the toes of his skis had crossed again. He got up patiently.

[56]

"That was his name," Ivar said.

"That was his name," Waino added.

"Maybe he'll come back," Jim Barry said, hopefully. He had never had a chance to see Honk.

Ivar shook his head. "No, he just came in and got a meal and went away again. He must have eaten enough to run him a month—even if somebody doesn't think he's a wild moose and shoot him."

"We can show Jim where he was," Waino suggested. "Let's all go down to the stable. It isn't quite supper-time."

When they got to the livery stable there were several men around Ivar's father's office. They were all talking and laughing.

"—and they all thought I was crazy," Mayor Olavsson was saying. "Well, I guess the town won't mind paying for his supper. How much do you think it was, Ivar?"

"Well," Ivar's father said, "about four horses. But I won't be too hard on you. A dollar and a half." He saw the boys and spoke to them. "Your mothers are probably looking for you."

"We just wanted to show Jim—" Ivar stopped and listened, and then he and Waino looked at each other.

Something was coming toward the stable "Clop-clop-clop" without any "cloppity" that an ordinary horse makes. A great, dark figure filled the front door of the stable and walked quickly over to Honk's stall. The men stared at each other but the boys yelled and hurried down the aisle.

"Honk!" they cried.

The moose looked a little uneasily at the men near the door and more uneasily at the boys running toward it. He tossed his head and started for the back door, but the back door was closed. The boys stopped. The moose turned and looked at them and suddenly they heard the men in the front shouting for them to come back.

"Honk!" said Ivar.

"HAWWWNNNKKK!" said the moose, too loudly.

"HONK!" said Ivar.

The moose waited for a while. "Haawwnnkk," he said more quietly and

[59]

began to walk back slowly. The boys retreated.

Honk smelled hay. He turned in at his regular stall and began to eat, glancing to the side from time to time. Ivar walked up slowly and patted him on the flank. Honk looked around. This was the little animal who had been there the night before when he discovered the good, loose grass. He couldn't be dangerous.

He said "HAWWNK" quite politely, and continued to eat hay.

The other two little things—one new—came up and began to pat him. It felt all right. The hay tasted good. Honk knew dimly that the little things had something to do with the loose grass—almost the only grass he'd found that winter. They were good little things, then.

He could almost understand them, too. They jumped around patting him and saying in almost moose language, "HONK—HONK—HONK."

His glance was quite friendly as he looked away from the hay now and then to be sure of them.

"Oh, my goodness," said Mr. Olavsson, "they're GLAD to see him—and HE'S glad to see THEM!"

Two of the boys were patting now, and Ivar was pulling down hay to Honk. When Honk reached too eagerly Ivar seized an edge of the great antlers and turned his head away.

"Dot's no moose—dot's a cocker spinach," said one of the bystanders.

"How did he get in?" Mr. Olavsson asked. "Why can't you keep him out?"

"I always leave the door open from 5:30 to 7—everybody comes then and I might be out for a sick cow or something."

"All right," Mr. Olavsson said solemnly. "People can get in doors that mooses don't know about. You keep him out tomorrow or the town won't pay any more."

Chapter VII

TOWN MOOSE

MONDAY was a school day. The boys reached the stable about four o'clock and found the big front doors closed on the latch; but when they had gone through the small door in the big door, there was no one in the stable but the horses.

Jim Barry laughed. "We can let him right in."

Ivar shook his head. "Papa would know."

They sat around and thought for a while and then Ivar had an idea. He whispered it and then he said: "The park would be the best place. Nobody goes there in the winter and there's lots of room for him."

There were lots of fat boys in Birora but in five minutes three of the fattest boys that had ever been seen anywhere slipped out of the *back* door of the livery stable. About ten minutes later the same three fat boys came out again and in ten minutes again.

They walked very curiously, waddling almost, in single file like Indians Every once in a while the front fat boy, Ivar, would dodge behind a tree and the others would dodge behind trees. Luckily they didn't meet anyone. At last they crept into safety among the trees of the city park, cold now, and swept by the wind, the flower beds all covered with straw.

In another five minutes Ivar, Waino and Jim came up to the *front* doors of the stable. "You know him best," Jim whispered. "You wait for him and we'll—" In five minutes only *two* of the fattest boys that had ever been seen crept out of the stable's back door.

Ivar was very uneasy while he waited. He didn't seem *very* fat now but Papa would be sure to notice. "Oh, come on, moose."

Once or twice he had to slip around the corner of the stable while men opened the doors and took their teams in. Of course, every one in Birora knew about Honk by now. All of the drivers shut the doors carefully as they went out, looked around and hurried home.

"Oh, come ON, moose—come on good old Honk!"

"Haawwnnkk!"

Ivar peered around the corner and saw Honk. "Thank goodness! You're awful late." Ivar reached under his mackinaw and pulled out a big handful of hay. "Come on, Honk."

[63]

By deserted back streets he led the animal down toward the park with its nailed-up bandstand. The wind was bitter cold but Honk didn't mind that as much as Ivar did. What Honk minded was never being able to get more than a nibble of hay at a time—the little thing would run at what was a fast walk for Honk for a few steps and surprisingly there would be another nibble of hay.

Then there was another of those flat tree things—it was the small room under the bandstand where they kept hoses and rakes and things for the park—and there was a great deal of loose grass and the other two little things who could almost speak Moose.

[64]

He liked the loose grass and he liked the three little things that were always around it. He ate a long time but, since he had now been well fed for three days, he wasn't sleepy. When the three little things decided to leave he didn't like it.

"HAAAWWWNNNKKK!"

Ivar turned on him. "Oh, my goodness, Honk!"

"You'll have the whole town down on us," Waino said.

Honk was quiet as soon as they came back. "You've got to keep quiet, you old moose! You don't know what would happen to you if they caught you down here." Ivar gave Honk a prod in the ribs which Honk accepted as a specially friendly pat.

The three boys were growing a little upset. It was supper-time and their mothers would be waiting for them. None of them wanted to make the others feel that he was a quitter, though.

They tried once more to slip out together, but in the meanwhile Honk had begun to grow more and more fond of the little things. Just as Ivar went out the door, Honk said, more feelingly and a good deal more loudly than before, "HAWWWWNNNNKKKK." For him it was warm under the bandstand, out of the wind, and he didn't want to go outside—he couldn't see why these little grass things would want to go out in the cold either.

"Now listen, Honk!" Ivar argued. "We've got to go to supper. Our folks are waiting for us. You stay here quiet and maybe we can come down a minute after supper."

Honk knew no English. His only reply was a pleased "Hawwnnkk" or two as the boys returned.

[65]

"Am I going to catch it when I get home?" Jim Barry asked, but he did not expect or need an answer.

"I'll tell you," Ivar said generously. "Honk knows Waino and me better than he knows you. You see if you can get away; and then, if you can, Waino can try it; and then, if he gets away, I'll sneak out somehow. He won't be nearly so likely to miss just one of us—anyhow, he might get sleepy pretty soon."

"I don't like to go away and leave you with him," Jim said.

"That's all right, Jim. He isn't really your moose yet anyway No use for all of us to get in trouble."

"Well—if you think you can manage him," Jim said, rather guiltily, and slid out of the bandstand. While he was leaving Ivar poked Honk in the ribs several times as hard as he could—he had learned that Honk liked this. The moose did indeed. He paid no attention to Jim.

"Well, that's one of us out," Ivar said, and sighed. "You're behind him, Waino—you better get away while you can." Ivar was scratching the moose's neck with both hands and Honk had turned his head and was looking at the boy with two sad, soft eyes—like two cups of beef broth.

"I'll wait for you outside," Waino said. He always stuck with Ivar. He slid out, and the moose kept on gazing at Ivar.

Ivar's hands grew tired. At last he got down on the floor and scratched together a little pile of hay that had been scattered. He pushed this off toward the side of the moose away from the door.

"Here's a bite you missed, Honk," he said very kindly and slid out into the darkness. Waino was waiting for him and the two boys stood for a moment listening. There was nothing but the sound of chewing.

[67]

"Let's get out of here," said Ivar, and they stole very slowly and carefully away.

At last they got to the sidewalk and started off briskly. They would just have time to stop at the livery stable to see that everything was all right before they ran home to their suppers.

They had gotten clear down to the main street before they noticed that the few people on the street were acting oddly. They were all going indoors. An automobile that had been coming toward them suddenly turned up on the sidewalk, backed quickly with a rasp of gears and dashed back the way it had come. A miner that they knew waved his arms at them, opened his mouth to shout and then turned and ran.

"What's the matter with them?" Waino asked curiously.

"Guess they can't stand the cold," Ivar said scornfully. Not being able to stand the cold is a terrible thing for a Suomi.

They could stand the cold. They threw back their shoulders and strutted down the street and around the corner to the livery stable. Ivar's father and the councilmen were sitting in the office, very much pleased with themselves.

"Well, I guess we got rid of him, all right," Ivar's father was saying for about the twentieth time.

"I guess we did," the Mayor said and he added thoughtfully: "Of course if it had been safe it might have been a good thing to keep him. A tame moose! Lots of summer vacation people might have come up to see him."

At this moment Ivar and Waino entered. Because he felt a little guilty, Ivar thought he should say something very innocent. "We're going right to supper, Papa—we didn't see how late it was."

[69]

"All right, son. You'd better hurry—" Ivar's father quit talking then and his mouth fell open. The councilmen turned and all of their mouths fell open, making five open mouths in all. And then, at last, Ivar and Waino turned and there were seven mouths open.

"Haawwnnkk!" said Honk, as much as to say, "Why did you run off from me?" and he curled his neck around like a big dog for Ivar to scratch.

"Well—I'll be frostbitten!" said Mayor Olavsson. "Put him in a stall Ivar, where he'll be safe. I guess this town is going to have a moose whether it wants one or not."

Chapter VIII

SPRING

THAT winter Honk made a record for his number of escapes. He would be found wandering down the main street looking with a good deal of interest at the people and the stores and forcing all the automobiles to the gutters and the sidewalks. Then Ivar and Waino had to be sent for, at school or anywhere, to get him in again.

At last the Mayor got Ivar's father to let the boys play with Honk in the park on Saturdays because he scared the potato farmers who drove in to town to trade that day. The policeman stood around to see that nothing happened, but by and by everyone got used to Honk and he got used to People so that no one was afraid of him any more. Honk got very fat and his hide shiny from the brushings the boys gave him.

In the first warm spell of the very early spring Mr. Pagnucco, the vegetable man, learned not to set his carrots and greens out on their sidewalk bins unless somebody was there to watch them. Honk liked carrots better than hay.

[72]

It grew a little more difficult toward spring when the farmers from the more distant farms began to come into Birora. A great many of them had never heard of Honk and got excited. One Finn farmer even fired both barrels of a shotgun at Honk and then went three miles and three-quarters—not as fast as he could, but as fast as he could without an airplane.

Honk didn't mind the little shot from a shotgun, though he didn't like the noise. He complained a little—"HAAWWNNKK!"—and the Finn farmer began hitting the ground every twenty feet instead of every ten.

He didn't understand why Marshal Ryan laughed after he telephoned.

Honk wasn't really angry. In fact, a few moments later Mrs. Zacklovich had to chase him out of her just sprouting corn with her apron. Honk considered the corn sprouts some of the very best grass he had ever eaten.

He was in serious disgrace for a few days the time he found the piece of candy in front of the grocery store. It was a nice, big piece of candy. He broke the crust around it with his hoof and licked at it until Mr. Millner came out and told him he was a bad moose. It was a hundred-pound sack of Mr. Millner's sugar that he had set outside for a customer. Honk "haw wnnkked" apologetically and went away sadly. He hadn't managed to finish the piece of candy.

Buds began to grow on the trees and the hills and swamps turned a light green. The snow melted off into patches. Honk spent more and more time out of the stable, grazing in the park and even on the edges of town, but he always came back to his stall to sleep.

One evening he didn't. The great spreading antlers had grown rusty gray and they seemed to itch. He scratched them on trees and even in the grass. He wandered farther and farther among the evergreen trees. It was spring and all his old friends were having a fine time out in the forests, eating the new tender grass.

The boys waited for him one night—two—three.

The fourth night Ivar, Waino and Jim went into the stable hopefully, but there was no sign of a moose.

Gone!

"Now *he's* run away from *us!*" Ivar said. "That's a moose for you!"

Chapter IX

WINTER

THE next winter was about the mildest winter the Range had ever seen—which isn't saying much for a country where it often gets to be thirty degrees below zero and sometimes fifty. This winter, however, there was plenty of moss, plenty of leaves, and the young moose were fat and happy, though many of the older moose had died the extra cold winter before.

[77]

The boys of Birora had had to give up skiing for snowballing. The snow was much too sticky for skis but it made splendid snow castles and very useful snowballs. Jim had a black eye from one.

Jim was a very good general. He had a red head and in snowballing this is almost ab-so-lute-ly ne-ces-sary to a general because when he jumps up on the edge of the fort and waves his hat the enemy can see clearly that he *is* the general and throw all their snowballs at him. After that the army advances.

It had been a very good day. They had driven Saari Karkes's army clear over the waste dump, from fort to fort, and at last he had had to give up his wooden sword, admitting that Jim's army was better than his until next Saturday. Jim didn't mind the black eye—he felt more natural with it. Ivar and Waino and Jim started home, up the brick streets.

"Well, g'bye, Ivar," Waino said, exactly as he had a year before. "I might as well turn in here."

"Oh, come down to the stable. We'll dry our boots and sit in the hay."

Waino thought it over. "All right. We'll plan how to fix our fort next Saturday."

He threw a snowball very accurately and hit a telephone pole. "Wish that had been—" And then he looked at Ivar with a very queer look. Both boys had a feeling that they remembered something that they couldn't quite remember.

"Gee," said Ivar slowly, "I wonder what's become of good old Honk."

"Gee," said Waino, "I wonder what's become of good old Honk."

"Yeah," said Jim.

Somewhat sadly they tramped on down to the stable.

[78]

At the stable there was a crowd of men—Ivar's father and Mr. Olavsson and Mr. Lunn and Mr. Ryan.

"Oh my goodness! Oh my goodness!" Ivar's father was saying.

But Mr. Olavsson only grinned. "He knows where the grass grows the thickest."

The boys didn't wait to hear any more. They rushed into the stable.

"Oh my goodness," Ivar's father said again. "What *will* the horses think—another winter?"

But from inside came out a thump of good loud kicks and the cheerful "Hawwnnkk" of a moose.

"Oh my goodness," Ivar's father said.

But from inside came a patter of leaping feet and a continued yelling of the boys' voices which by and by took up a regular rhythm—

"HONK! HONK! GOOD OLD HONK!"